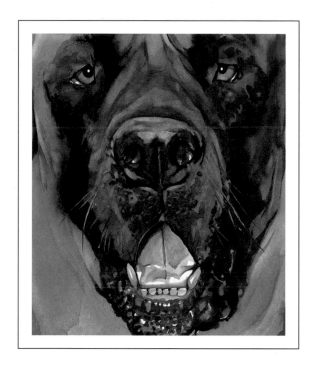

# Sit, Truman!

# Sit, Truman!

DAN HARPER

*Illustrated by*
*Cara Moser & Barry Moser*

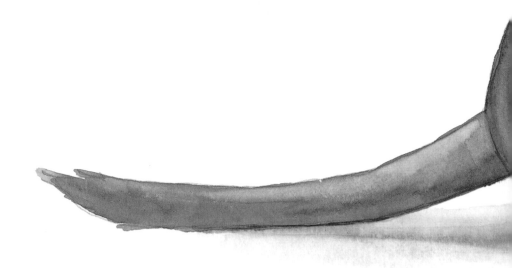

VOYAGER BOOKS · HARCOURT, INC.

*Orlando   Austin   New York   San Diego   Toronto   London*

Truman, sit!

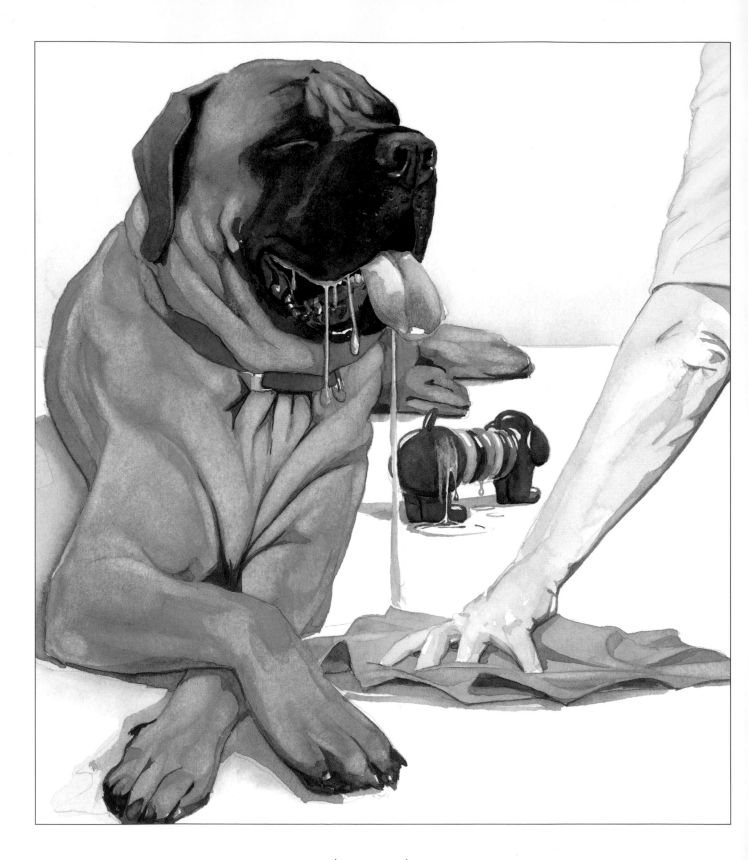

Truman, stop drooling.

Truman, Oscar is *not* a toy.

Truman, that is not your water bowl…

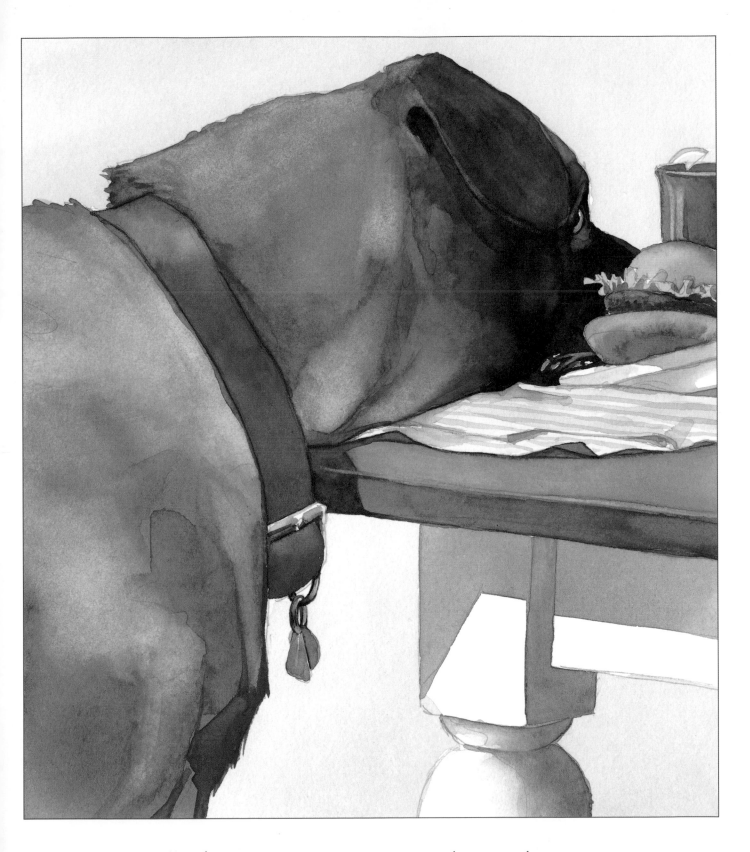

...and *that* is not your lunch!

Share, Truman, share.

Truman, no dancing.

Okay, okay, let's go!

No, Truman, we're walking.

Sorry, Truman, nothing for you.

Truman, heel!

Go get it, Truman!

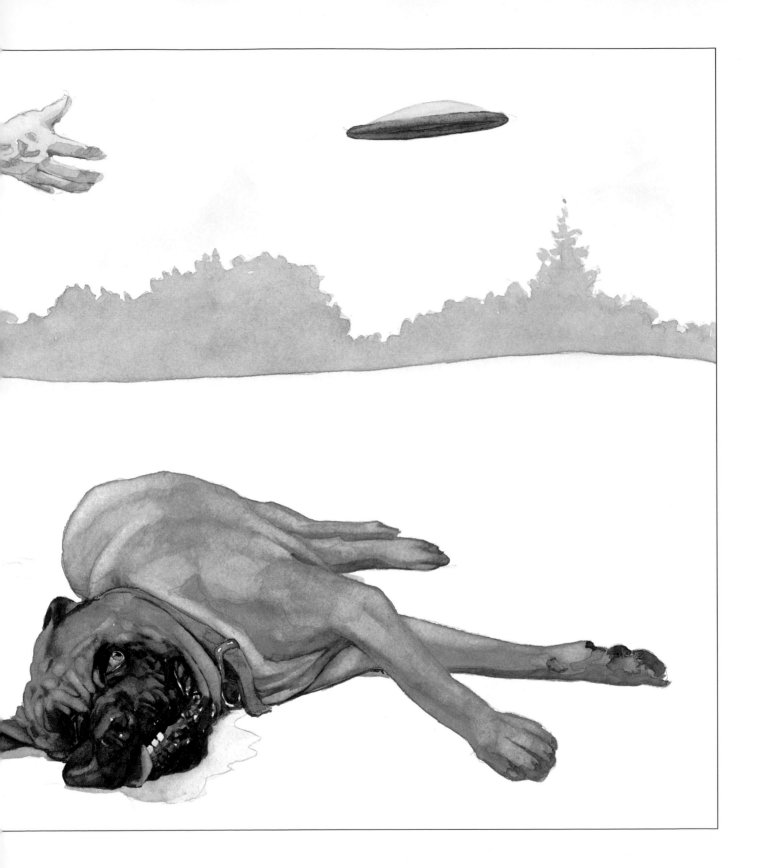

Time to go.

No snacks today, Truman.

Truman, that's Oscar's bed…

...and this is *my* bed!

Did you brush, Truman?

Truman, be nice.

Good boy, Truman!

*For Mom and Pop, with thanks for everything*—D. H.

*For all the people who live with dogs that drool on a grand scale—*
*with great sympathy*—C. M. & B. M.

www.HarcourtBooks.com

The Library of Congress has cataloged the hardcover edition as follows:
Harper, Dan, 1963–
Sit, Truman!/written by Dan Harper; illustrated by Cara Moser and Barry Moser.
p. cm.
Summary: A busy day in the life of Truman the dog includes walks, play time, and a little dog named Oscar.
[1. Dogs—Fiction.] I. Moser, Cara, ill. II. Moser, Barry, ill. III. Title.
PZ7.H231325Si 2001 [E]—dc21 00-9298
ISBN 0-15-202616-9
ISBN 0-15-205068-X pb

A C E G H F D B

The illustrations in this book were composed by Cara Moser and then translated by
Barry Moser into transparent watercolor paintings on various handmade papers.
The title was hand lettered by Judythe Sieck.
The text type was set in Requiem.
Color separations by Bright Arts Ltd., Hong Kong
Printed and bound by Tien Wah Press, Singapore
Production supervision by Sandra Grebenar and Ginger Boyer
Designed by Cara Moser, Barry Moser, and Judythe Sieck